CU00868336

# The Red Sneakers

Kristin Laubenthal

AuthorHouse™
1663 Liberty Drive
Bloomington, IN 47403
www.authorhouse.com
Phone: 1 (800) 839-8640

© 2019 Kristin Laubenthal. All rights reserved.

No part of this book may be reproduced, stored in a retrieval system, or transmitted
by any means without the written permission of the author.

Published by AuthorHouse 07/31/2019

ISBN: 978-1-7283-2177-6 (sc)
ISBN: 978-1-7283-2178-3 (hc)
ISBN: 978-1-7283-2176-9 (e)

Print information available on the last page.

Any people depicted in stock imagery provided by Getty Images are models,
and such images are being used for illustrative purposes only.
Certain stock imagery © Getty Images.

This book is printed on acid-free paper.

Because of the dynamic nature of the Internet, any web addresses or links contained in this book may have changed
since publication and may no longer be valid. The views expressed in this work are solely those of the author and do
not necessarily reflect the views of the publisher, and the publisher hereby disclaims any responsibility for them.

authorHOUSE®

Zoe rushed around her room, getting her school bag ready. Then she started on her first-day-of-school outfit.

"Mom," she yelled, "where are my new red sneakers?"

"Zoe, what are you doing?" said Mom.

Pausing a moment, Zoe looked up. "My brand-new sneakers. The ones I LOVE. My first-day-of-school sneakers … I can't find them!"

"We put them under your bed, remember," Mom said, pointing.

"Oh, yeah." Zoe leapt to the bed, grabbed the sneakers, and twirled around. "Thanks, Mom. Now, I'm all ready for tomorrow."

Zoe walked into class with her head high. She had a new first-day outfit, but all she cared about was her new red sneakers.

"Wow, Zoe. Cool sneakers," said Natasha.

"Yeah," said Julia, "way cool." Looking toward the door, Julia narrowed her eyes. "Who's that?"

A new girl walked in. Her clothes were worn and her old sneakers had holes in them.

"Good morning, Annabelle," said Ms. Kelly. She led the new girl to a desk near the front of the class and gave her supplies.

"She looks awful," said Natasha. "And, she doesn't even have her own supplies."

Julia squished up her face. "I'm glad she's not sitting next to me."

The rest of the morning, all the children in the class talked about the new girl. Instead of making her feel welcome, they made fun of her.

Annabelle looks so sad, thought Zoe. Why are they being mean to her?

During lunch, everyone stayed far away from Annabelle ... everyone except Zoe.

"Hi, I'm Zoe." She sat down next to Annabelle.

"H-Hi," said Annabelle, almost whispering. She put one foot over the other.

Zoe knew Annabelle was trying to hide her sneakers. "So, how's your first day going?"

Annabelle shrugged. "It's tough going to a new school, especially when you're d-different. My parents can't afford to get me new clothing or school supplies."

Zoe felt something she'd never felt before. She felt sad because Annabelle didn't have anything new for the first day of school.

She looked at her recess-sneakers that were in a bag. "Hey," said Zoe, "Would you mind taking my sneakers. My mom got me red ones, but I like my old ones a lot better."

Annabelle stared at Zoe's red sneakers. "I-I couldn't. What would your mom say?"

With her elbow on the table and her head in her hand, Zoe scrunched up her face. "I know she won't care."

During recess, Julia and Natasha rushed over to Zoe. "Why does Annabelle have your new sneakers?" asked Julia.

Annabelle lowered her head.

"I asked Annabelle to take my sneakers. I like my old ones so much better."

Julia and Natasha walked away giggling and whispering. Soon, everyone was giggling and whispering.

"I didn't think this would be a good idea," said Annabelle. "They're all making fun of us." She sat down and took off the red sneakers.

At home, Zoe didn't eat her snack. "What's wrong, sweetie?" asked Mom.

"It's a new girl at school," said Zoe. "She wasn't dressed nice and didn't have the school supplies. Everyone made fun of her."

Mom shook her head. "That's terrible."

"I felt awful for her. I gave her my new sneakers, but the children made fun of both of us. So, she took them off."

"I'm sorry," said Mom. "But I'm proud that you didn't follow the crowd. What you feel is called empathy. It's when you can understand how someone is feeling."

"Was it okay that I gave her my sneakers?"

"Well, Zoe, you should always ask me or your father before giving something away, but if you had, I would have said, of course."

In class, the teacher went over the math test they had the day before. Then she handed back the test papers. "Congratulations, Annabelle. You got a hundred!"

Zoe looked at her paper. "Hmph. I guess seventy is okay." She looked over to Julia. "What'd you get?"

Julia shoved the paper in her notebook. "It's not a hundred," she grumbled.

"It seems many of you need help with the new math," said Ms. Kelly. "We'll have afterschool help starting next week."

Natasha folded her arms. "I don't want to stay after school."

"Me either," said Zoe. "Hey, I have an idea."

When the school bell rang, Zoe rushed over to Annabelle. "I need your help with the new math. And, so do a few other children. Would you be willing to help us?"

Annabelle looked past Zoe at Julia, Natasha, Shaun, and Christian. "I guess."

"Super!" said Zoe as she twirled around the room. "Each day during recess, we'll go over the math."

And, each day they did.

By the end of the
week, Ms. Kelly gave
another test and the
students Annabelle
helped got much
better grades.

During lunch, Zoe and the other children sat with Annabelle.

"You helped us even though you didn't have to, so we'd like to do something nice for you," said Zoe.

ulia gave Annabelle a new notebook and pencil.

Natasha gave Annabelle a new ruler, scotch tape, and a compass.

Shaun gave Annabelle two new binders.

Christian gave Annabelle a new picture book.

Zoe gave Annabelle a box.

Tears welled up in Annabelle's eyes. "The red sneakers. I-I can't"

"Yes, you can!" said all the children.

"I talked to my mom," said Zoe, "and she said we should help each other."

"And, we're sorry," said Julia, "for not being kind on your first day."

"Thank you all," said Annabelle.

When they went out for recess, Annabelle jumped and danced around. "These sneakers are amazing!"

A warm feeling started in Zoe's belly and spread through her body. She smiled inside and out.

CPSIA information can be obtained
at www.ICGtesting.com
Printed in the USA
BVHW021651060819
555211BV00010B/143/P

9 781728 321783